THE RABBIT AND BEAR BOOKS:

RABBIT & BEAR

Rabbit's Bad Habits

STORY BY
JULIAN GOUGH

ILLUSTRATIONS BY
JIM FIELD

h
Hodder
Children's
Books

HODDER CHILDREN'S BOOKS

First published in hardback in Great Britain in 2016 by Hodder Children's Books
This paperback edition published in 2016

16

Text copyright © Julian Gough, 2016
Illustrations copyright © Jim Field, 2016

The moral rights of the author and illustrator have been asserted.

A CIP catalogue record for this book
is available from the British Library.

ISBN 978 1 444 92168 7

Printed and bound in China

The paper and board used in this book are from
well-managed forests and other responsible sources.

Hodder Children's Books
An imprint of
Hachette Children's Group
Part of Hodder and Stoughton
Carmelite House
50 Victoria Embankment
London EC4Y 0DZ

An Hachette UK Company
www.hachette.co.uk
www.hachettechildrens.co.uk

In memory of the forever smiling Julie Crosbie

J.F.

●

Dedicated to my daughter, Sophie. She helped me to write the story, and rewrite it, over many, many drafts. She laughed at the good bits, frowned at the bad bits, and, at one point (while I was reading her the latest version of a funny scene), burst into tears.
"What's wrong?" I asked, rather worried.
"You've taken out ..." she sobbed, "... my *favourite line!*"
She was quite right, I realised; and so I put it back in.
(It's the line, spoken by Wolf, "I'm sick of having my dinner run away from me at forty miles an hour.")
Now, THAT'S a passionate and committed editor ...
Thank you, Sophie.

J.G.

As the robber left the cave,
he stood on Bear's nose. Bear
woke up.

"My honey! My salmon!
And my delicious beetles'
eggs!" said Bear. "Gone!"

But outside, in the snowstorm, there was no sign of the robber, or the food.

Snowstorm? thought Bear. SNOWSTORM?!? This isn't Spring ... I've woken up early! Oh well. I've always wanted to make a snowman.

The storm ended.

Bear rolled a snowball all the way down her hill, and up to the top of the next. She sat down, panting.

"It's the end of the world,"
said a gloomy voice.

Bear looked all around. "No it
isn't," said Bear cautiously. "It's a
lovely sunny day."

"Nonsense!" said
the voice, from below.
"The sun's gone out."

Ah, thought Bear. She rolled
her snowball sideways, and
uncovered a rabbit hole.

Rabbit popped out. He
looked at Bear. He looked at
the giant snowball.

"Only an idiot," said Rabbit thoughtfully,
"rolls a snowball UP a hill ..."
"Why?" said Bear.

"Gravity."

"What's Gravity?" said Bear.

"Gravity," said Rabbit rather importantly, "Is the Mysterious Force which Attracts Everything to Everything Else."

"Ah!" said Bear, nodding.
"Like Friendship."
   "No!" said Rabbit.
   "Love?" said Bear.
   "No!! No!!"
said Rabbit.

"Oh ... Hunger?" said Bear,
who was feeling mysteriously
attracted to the idea of breakfast.

"No!!! No!!! No!!!" said Rabbit, and
shoved Bear's giant snowball as hard
as he could. It rolled down the hill, faster
and faster, getting bigger as it went,
and skidded across the frozen
lake till the ice cracked. Bear's
snowball disappeared ...

with a

PLOP

Bear's mouth
opened in shock.
"See?" said Rabbit
triumphantly. "Gravity
WANTS you to push snow
DOWN a hill, and will help
you. But Gravity does
NOT want you to push
snow UP a hill, and will
try to stop you. And only a
fool," said Rabbit severely,
"picks a fight with Gravity."

Bear finally closed her mouth, sighed, and began to roll another snowball. "You know an awful lot about Gravity," she said.

"I am an Expert," said
Rabbit. "Gravity nearly killed
my Grandfather. Now, if you
could do me a favour ..."

"I'd be delighted," said Bear.

Rabbit nodded. "Go away,"
he said. "And take your
Avalanche with you."

"What," said Bear cautiously, "is an Avalanche?"

"An Avalanche," said Rabbit, pointing at the snowball Bear was rolling, "is a huge load of snow that rolls down a mountain faster than a train. My Grandfather was buried in an Avalanche. He had to eat his own leg to survive, while he was waiting for them to dig him out."

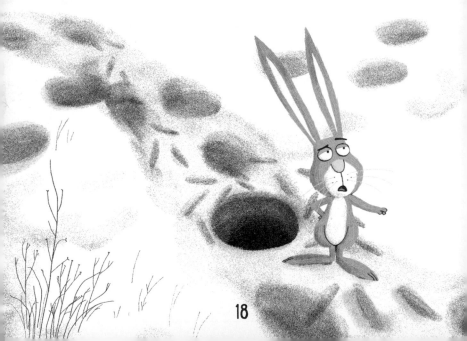

18

"Really?" said Bear, impressed. "He must have been buried for a very long time."

"Well, no," said Rabbit. "About ten minutes. But he was very hungry. We get VERY VERY hungry in our family."

Bear's stomach rumbled.

"Oh yes," said Rabbit.
"I'd forgotten. You haven't
any food."

"How did you know?"
said Bear.

But Rabbit was gone.
He soon reappeared.
"No hard feelings," said
Rabbit. "Here." And he
handed Bear the oldest,
saddest, floppiest,
blackest carrot Bear had
ever seen. "You can eat it.
Or use it as a nose for your
Snowy Man."

Bear sniffed the black, floppy carrot. Ugh.
"Er, nose, I think ..." said Bear. "Would you
like to help me build my Snowman?"

Rabbit thought for a second. "No,"
he said.

Bear sighed, turned, and
rolled her snowball back down
Rabbit's hill. By the time she'd
got it back up her own hill, it
was bigger than the first one.
Perfect, thought Bear, panting.
She started to make a head.
Pretty soon she was singing.

Rabbit could hear Bear's song from his burrow.

"Hmm," said Rabbit. "Making a snowman DOES seem to be ..." Rabbit had trouble saying the next word, because he'd never used it before. "F ... f ... f ... f ... fun ... Hah! I shall make an even BETTER snowman." But first, for energy, Rabbit ate lots and lots AND LOTS of the honey, and frozen salmon, and delicious beetles' eggs, that he'd stolen off Bear during the storm.

27

Then he did a little poo, and ate it.

This rather embarrassing habit
was the reason Rabbit never invited
people over for tea.

"I forgot to say thanks
for the carrot," said Bear's
voice, right behind Rabbit.
"Aaarkk!" Rabbit
jumped his own height in
fright and scrambled out
of the burrow. "Oh. Bear
… You're welcome …"

31

"I say Rabbit, did you just eat your own poo?" said Bear, wondering if she'd seen right.

"Ah," said Rabbit. "Yes. A little bit."

"A little bit of YOUR OWN POO?" asked Bear, wondering if she'd heard right.

"Shush!" said Rabbit, glancing around. "Look, all rabbits do it. It's perfectly normal."

"For a rabbit, maybe," said Bear.

"Well," said Rabbit, drawing himself up to his full height, which gave him a good view of Bear's tummy, "I'm sure bears do some things in the woods that they wouldn't like to talk about."

"But WHY do rabbits eat their poo?"
said Bear.

"Well, why do YOU eat?"
said Rabbit.

"Um, to get Energy.
And to make new
bits of Bear."

"Exactly," said Rabbit. "It's easy to make a bear out of honey, salmon, and delicious beetles' eggs. They're full of energy. It's easy to make a wolf out of meat. FULL of energy. But it's really, really difficult to make a rabbit out of plants."

"Why?" said Bear.

"Because when you've eaten the plants, and digested them in your tummy for hours, and pooed them ... the job is only half done!"

"No energy?" said Bear.

"None!" said Rabbit. "The energy is still trapped in the poo! It's sort of soft and black, like licorice ..."

"Yes, yes," said Bear hastily.

"So you have to eat your own poo," said Rabbit, "and digest it ALL OVER AGAIN, to get the energy out."

"Really?" said Bear. For some reason she wasn't hungry any more.

"Yes," said Rabbit. "And THEN you have to poo a totally DIFFERENT kind of poo ... sort of a dry, brown poo, with just the grassy, twiggy bits in ..."

Bear felt a little weak. "So, um, er ... do rabbits eat the other kind of poo?" she said.

"What?" said Rabbit. He couldn't quite believe his enormous ears.

"The dry brown
ones, with the
grassy twiggy bits
in," Bear added
helpfully.

"Eat the other kind of poo?" said Rabbit. "EAT THE OTHER KIND OF POO? That's DISGUSTING!"

"Oh good," said Bear. "Just checking."

"From dawn to dusk, you're eating and pooing," said Rabbit gloomily.

"And half the time you're eating poo. It's an awful life."

"Maybe that's why you're so grumpy,"
said Bear.

"Grumpy?" said Rabbit. "I'm not
GRUMPY!"

"OK, you're not grumpy," said Bear.
"Well, I'm off to, er ... wash my carrot."

45

I hate being a
rabbit, thought Rabbit,
and popped down the
burrow to eat more of
Bear's food.

Then, full of energy, Rabbit got back to
work on his snowman. Soon he had rolled a
huge snowball right over his burrow.

"What a lovely little head!" shouted Bear
from her hilltop. "Thanks! But I've already
made one!"

"It's not a head," said Rabbit, furious.
"And it's not for you! It's a body! I've only
started! And it'll be much bigger than
yours! Eventually!"

Bear gasped.

"Why," said Rabbit, irritated, "are you gasping? Don't you believe me?"

"I am gasping," shouted Bear politely, "because you are about to be eaten by Wolf."

Rabbit looked over his shoulder.

49

Wolf was bounding towards
him across the snow.

Gosh, Wolf had a lot of teeth.
And Rabbit's snowball blocked his burrow.

50

"Aaaarrk! Splfff!
Waaahhh!" said Rabbit,
and turned and ran ...

51

Oh dear, thought Bear. Rabbit gave me a carrot ... so he's my friend ...

Bear made a snowball, and
threw it, with all her Bear's strength.
It went over Wolf's head and landed on the
frozen lake. Crack. Plop. Whoops …

Bear made a second snowball, and threw
it, with a lot less of her Bear's strength. It fell
not very far from Bear.

Bear frowned. She made a third
snowball, and threw it, with just
the right amount of her Bear's
strength. It landed on Wolf's
head, right between his ears.

THUD!

Far below, Wolf skidded to a halt,
shouted, "You keep out of this!" to Bear,
and raced on again after Rabbit. Bear
sighed. No, to stop Wolf you'd need a
snowball as big as an Avalanche,
and as fast as a Train …

Hmm. Wait.

Bear knocked off her Snow Man's head, and sent it rolling down the hill, towards where Wolf was going to be in about a minute.

Bear was actually a lot cleverer than she thought she was.

Rabbit, as he ran,
looked over his
shoulder at Wolf, and
his eyes opened wide.
"Look behind you!"
gasped Rabbit.

61

"I'm not falling for that," panted Wolf. Hmm, he did hear a noise behind him all right. No, he wasn't going to look, it was a trick. "That's just another of Bear's snowballs."

"Well, it is – and it isn't," said Rabbit.

He tried to remember what his three-legged grandfather had said about Avalanches. Oh yes, it's a good idea to GET OUT OF THE WAY of them.

"Ah, that was it," panted Rabbit, and jumped sideways.

"WHAT was it?" panted Wolf, and the noise was so loud now that he finally looked over his shoulder.

He didn't even have time to gasp. A snowball the size of an avalanche hit Wolf faster than a train, and rolled him out on to the thin ice of the lake. The ice cracked.

By the time Wolf had crawled ashore, Rabbit was half a mile away.

Wolf snorted. Owch. There was something stuck up his nose. He sneezed.

Out popped the old, black, floppy carrot. Wolf sniffed it. Ugh.

Still, he rather liked the way it just sat there.

SNIFF

"Hmmm. Maybe I'll go vegetarian for a bit," said Wolf. "I'm sick of having my dinner run away from me at forty miles an hour."

68

Wolf gave the
carrot a bite.

BLuuuuuuuHH!

Uggy uggy uggy! Bluuuuuuhh!
Wolf spat the old, black,
floppy carrot back into the lake.

He sighed, licked his huge, sharp teeth, and went home to dry off.

"Bear," said Rabbit, "why did you save me when I was so mean to you?"

"Because you gave me a carrot," said Bear.

"But it was an old, black, floppy carrot," said Rabbit.

"It's the thought that counts," said Bear.

Rabbit blushed, and ran off.

Oh well, thought
Bear, I suppose
he's gone to Eat.
Or Poo. Or eat poo.

But he hadn't.

Back home, Rabbit pushed the body of his snowman until it rolled down his hill, and halfway up Bear's.

"Bear!" shouted Rabbit. "Help me push this snowball up your hill."

When they'd got it to the top, Rabbit panted, "It's a present ... for your Snow Man."

They heaved
the new head
on to the body.
Bear did most of
the heaving, as
Rabbit couldn't
reach that high.

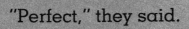

"Perfect," they said.

Bear carefully pushed two pine cones into
the head, for eyes.

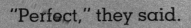
"Perfect," they said.

Rabbit picked up a curved stick, jumped as high as he could, and slapped a mouth on the Snowman.

"Perfect," said Rabbit.

"Hmmmmm," said Bear.

The stick unstuck, and fell off.

Bear turned it upside down, and carefully put it back on, so that it made a smile.

"Perfect," they said together.

"I'm afraid I lost the carrot that you gave me," said Bear.

Rabbit smiled, for the first time ever. It hardly hurt at all. He reached behind him. "Ta-dah!" Rabbit gave his best and brightest orange carrot to Bear. "For your Snow Man."

"No," said Bear.
"No?" said Rabbit, shocked.

"For OUR Snow Man," said Bear, and carefully pushed the carrot nose into the Snow Man's head.

"Perfect," they said together.

"So," said Rabbit, happily. "Tomorrow we could meet up, and play, and ..."

"Sorry," said Bear. "I'm really hungry, and I've no food. I'll have to go back to sleep till winter is over ..."

Rabbit smiled. It was even easier the second time. He produced a honeycomb from behind his back. And a frozen salmon. And some delicious beetles' eggs.

"But ... but ... this is just like the food I
had!" Bear said.

"It IS the food you had," said Rabbit. "I'm
sorry I stole it. You can have it all back."

"But then YOU
won't have any
food," said Bear.
"I don't think
I deserve any,"
said Rabbit, very
quietly.

"Well … look here, Rabbit," said Bear. "You don't like being a rabbit anyway. Why not stay in my cave, and be a bear, with me?"

"Perfect!" said Rabbit.

"Let's have a moonlight picnic to celebrate!" said Bear.

It was a long and lovely picnic. Bear had built up a wonderful appetite, after sleeping half the winter, and Rabbit was, as usual, VERY, VERY hungry.

Rabbit looked out the mouth of the warm cave, at the Snow Man glittering in the moonlight.

"He looks a little lonely, out there in the cold," said Rabbit.

"In the morning," murmured Bear,
"we can make him a Friend."
And Rabbit and Bear fell asleep
together in their warm cave.

Outside, the Snow Man

smiled in the moonlight.

LOOK OUT FOR MORE

RABBIT
& BEAR

BOOKS COMING SOON!

FIND OUT WHAT HAPPENS NEXT IN:

The Pest
in the Nest

Rabbit's Bad Habits is a breath of fresh air in children's fiction, a laugh-out-loud story of rabbit and wolf and bear, of avalanches and snowmen. The sort of story that makes you want to send your children to bed early, so you can read it to them.'
Neil Gaiman

'A perfect animal double-act enchants.'
Alex O'Connell, *The Times* book of the week

'Sure to become a firm favourite.'
The Bookbag

'What a treat this little book is! Not only does it have a funny and warm story that is full of heart, it is also gorgeously presented... Lots of fun, highly recommended.'
Reading Zone